CANARY COTTAGE
SHEEP PEN
N
W
E
S
MOLE'S HOUSE
RAT'S HOUSE
OSIER BED
OTTERS HOUSE
PAN ISLAND
THE WEIR
AF729821

PRIVATE
NO LANDING
ALLOWED

Messing About on the River

The *Wind in the Willows*, first published by Methuen & Co 1908,
with E.H.Shepard illustrations 1931
Published in this format 2026 by Farshore
An imprint of HarperCollins*Publishers*
1 London Bridge Street, London SE1 9GF
www.farshore.co.uk

HarperCollins*Publishers*
Macken House, 39/40 Mayor Street Upper,
Dublin 1, D01 C9W8, Ireland

Text by Kenneth Grahame

978 0 00 880310 0

1

Printed in Malaysia

A CIP catalogue record for this title is available from the British Library.

Messing About on the River

Mindful moments from
The Wind in the Willows

With decorations by
E.H.Shepard

Spring was moving in the air above and in the earth below and around him, penetrating even his dark and lowly little house with its spirit of divine discontent and longing.

SPRING IS NATURE'S WAY OF TELLING US THAT HOPE IS JUST AROUND THE CORNER.

The carol of happy birds
fell on his dulled hearing
almost like a shout.

BIRD SONG IS A LULLABY THAT CAN SOOTHE THE MOST TROUBLED SOUL.

After all, the best part of a holiday is perhaps not so much to be resting yourself, as to see all the other fellows busy working.

IT'S OKAY TO TAKE A
MOMENT TO STEP BACK,
JUST SO THAT YOU CAN
MOVE FORWARD AGAIN.

The river still
chattered on to him,
a babbling procession

of the best stories
in the world,

sent from the heart
of the earth
to be told at last to
the insatiable sea.

A STORY CAN
TAKE YOU
ANYWHERE
YOU WANT
TO GO.

"What's inside it?" asked the Mole, wriggling with curiosity.

THERE ARE VERY FEW SURPRISES
LEFT IN LIFE, SO EMBRACE THEM
WHEN THEY COME!

Absorbed in the new life he was entering upon, intoxicated with the sparkle, the ripple, the scents and the sounds and the sunlight, he trailed a paw in the water and dreamt long waking dreams. The Water Rat, like the good little fellow he was, sculled steadily on and forebore to disturb him.

THE BEST FRIENDS ARE THE ONES WE CAN SIT WITH IN COMFORTABLE SILENCE.

"O MY! O MY! O MY!"

TREASURE EVERY LITTLE MOMENT
OF JOY, THEY ADD UP TO A
LIFETIME OF HAPPINESS.

"It's my world,

and I don't want any other.

What it hasn't got is not worth having,

and what it doesn't know is not

worth knowing."

THERE IS REAL PEACE
IN KNOWING
YOU'RE RIGHT
WHERE YOU'RE
MEANT
TO BE.

LOOK UP ONCE IN A WHILE,
LIFE GOES BY SO QUICKLY.

"I am looking," said the Mole,
"at a streak of bubbles that I see
travelling along the surface of the water.
That is a thing that strikes me as funny."

TAKE GREAT PLEASURE IN THE
LITTLE THINGS IN LIFE.

TRY,

TRY,

TRY AGAIN.

The Rat made a bright fire in the parlour, and planted the Mole in an arm-chair in front of it, having fetched down a dressing-gown and slippers for him, and told him river stories till supper-time.

SOMETIMES
THE SMALLEST GESTURES
CAN MAKE US FEEL LOVED
AND CARED FOR IN
THE **BIGGEST** WAY.

Mole soon
laid his head
on his pillow
in great
peace and
contentment,
knowing that
his new-found
friend the River
was lapping
the sill
of his
window.

IF THE LAND OF NOD
SEEMS FAR AWAY,
LET THE SOUND
OF WATER LULL
YOU THERE.

"Get the boat out,
and we'll paddle up there
at once. It's never the
wrong time to call on Toad.
Always good tempered,
always glad to see you,
always sorry when you go!"

YOUR FRIENDS KNOW
WHAT MAKES YOU
WONDERFUL.

VATE
LANDING
OWED

TO PLAN TO TRAVEL,
IS TO OPEN UP TO
EVERY POSSIBILITY OF
HAPPINESS.

"There you are!" cried the Toad, straddling and expanding himself. "There's real life for you, embodied in that little cart."

REAL HAPPINESS
DOESN'T LIE IN
THE DESTINATION
BUT THE JOURNEY
ITSELF.

DON'T BE AFRAID TO CHASE WHAT MIGHT SEEM OUT OF REACH.

After so much open air and excitement the Toad slept very soundly, and no amount of shaking could rouse him out of bed next morning.

THERE'S NOTHING LIKE FRESH
COUNTRY AIR TO HELP YOU GET
A DEEP AND RESTFUL SLEEP!

"Glorious, stirring sight!" murmured Toad, never offering to move. "The poetry of motion!"

ALWAYS LOOK ON THE
BRIGHT SIDE OF LIFE.

"I owe it all to you,
my best of friends!"

GOOD FRIENDS WILL ALWAYS
CATCH YOU WHEN YOU FALL.

In the wintertime the Rat slept a great deal, retiring early and rising late. There was a good deal of story-telling and comparing notes on the past summer and all its doings.

THE CHANGING OF THE SEASONS IS A REASSURING CONSTANT IN OUR HECTIC AND UNPREDICTABLE LIVES.

Mole thought that he had never seen so far and so intimately into the inside of things as on that winter day when Nature was deep in her annual slumber.

YOU CAN ALWAYS FIND BEAUTY IN WHATEVER LIES BEFORE YOU IF YOUR EYES AND HEART ARE TRULY OPEN.

His paper of half-finished
verses slipped from his knee,
his head fell back, his mouth
opened, and he wandered by the
verdant banks of dream-rivers.

THERE ARE FEW PLEASURES
AS COMFORTING AS A
CRACKLING FIRE ON A COLD
WINTER'S EVENING.

"Dear Ratty," said the poor Mole, "I'm dreadfully sorry, but I'm simply dead beat and that's a solid fact. You must let me rest here a while longer and get my strength back."

SET YOUR BOUNDARIES AND PRACTISE SELF-CARE. YOU'RE WORTH IT!

Suddenly the Rat cried

"Hooray!"

and then

"Hooray-oo-ray-oo-ray-oo-ray!"

CELEBRATE ALL OF LIFE'S WINS!

“Ring hard as you can
while I hammer!”

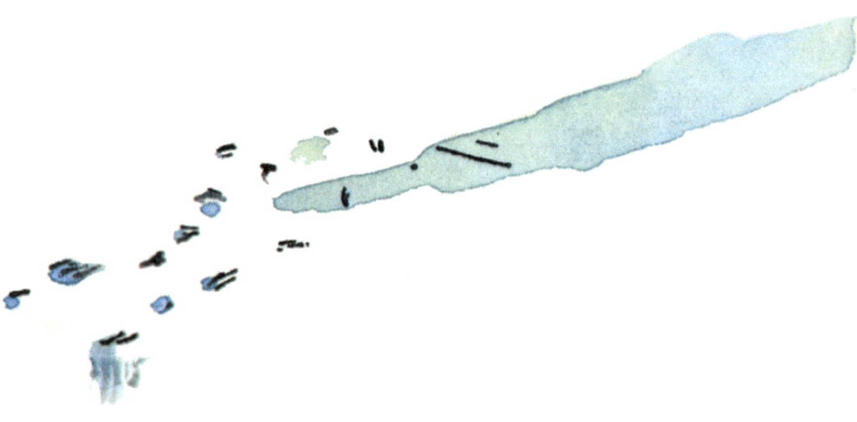

GOOD FRIENDS ARE WORTH BEATING
DOWN THE DOOR FOR!

"Come along in, both of you, at once.

Why you must be perished.

Well I never! Lost in the snow!"

NOTHING MEANS MORE THAN THE COMFORT OF A WARM WELCOME AFTER BEING OUT IN THE COLD.

"Now then! Tell us the news from your part of the world. How's old Toad going on?"

SOMETIMES IN LIFE, ALL YOU NEED IS GOOD FOOD, GOOD FRIENDS AND GOOD CONVERSATION.

"Where have you youngsters come from? Lost your way in the snow, I suppose?"

WITHOUT THE MISTAKES OF OUR YOUTH,
WE WOULDN'T BE THE STRONGER
AND WISER PEOPLE WE ARE TODAY.

BEHIND EVERY
CLOSED DOOR
IS A CHANCE
TO DISCOVER
SOMETHING OR
SOMEONE NEW.

"The master's gone into his study, sir," replied the hedgehog, "and he said as how he was going to be particular busy this morning, and on no account was he to be disturbed."

MAKE SPACE FOR
ALONE TIME AWAY
FROM EVERYONE ELSE'S
THOUGHTS SO THAT YOU
CAN SPEND TIME WITH
YOUR OWN.

"It'll be all right, my fine fellow," said the Otter. "I'm coming along with you."

YOU NEVER HAVE TO
WALK IN ANOTHER'S
FOOTPRINTS BUT
THERE IS MUCH
TO BE SAID FOR
MAKING YOUR OWN
WITH SOMEONE
BY YOUR SIDE.

Little was visible but squares of a dusky orange-red on either side of the street, where the firelight or lamplight of each cottage overflowed through the casements into the dark world without.

HOWEVER DARK THE WORLD MAY SEEM, THERE WILL ALWAYS BE A GLIMMER OF LIGHT TO GUIDE YOU HOME.

"It's my home, my old home! I've just come across the smell of it, and it's close by here, really quite close. And I must go to it, I must, I must!"

HOME IS WHERE THE HEART IS.

"No bread!" groaned the Mole dolorously; "no butter, no –"

"No pâté de foie gras, no champagne!" continued the Rat grinning.

IT'S NOT WHAT YOU HAVE IN LIFE,
IT'S WHO YOU'RE WITH
THAT REALLY MATTERS.

"I think it must be the field-mice," replied the Mole. "They go round carol-singing regularly at this time of the year. I used to give them hot drinks, and supper too sometimes, when I could afford it. It will be like old times to hear them again."

THERE IS INFINITELY MORE JOY IN THE ACT OF GIVING THAN THE PLEASURE OF RECEIVING.

A hot sun seemed to be pulling everything green and bushy and spiky up out of the earth as if by strings. The Mole and the Water Rat had been up since dawn, very busy on matters concerned with boats.

FIND A SENSE OF PEACE AND MINDFULNESS IN THE DOING OF SIMPLE EVERYDAY TASKS.

"Hullo come on, you fellows!"
Toad cried cheerfully.

ALWAYS BE THE LIGHT.

"Now, then!" Badger said
to Toad, "first of all take
those ridiculous things off!"
"Shan't!" replied Toad,
with great spirit.

EMBRACE YOUR OWN STYLE
AND WEAR IT PROUDLY.

"Dear, kind Rat," murmured Toad, "how little you realize my condition, and how very far I am from 'jumping up' now – if ever!"

IT'S OKAY NOT TO BE OKAY.

THE WORLD IS FULL OF ADVENTURE — ALL YOU HAVE TO DO IS GO OUT AND FIND IT!

"O, the blessed coolness!"

THE PERFECT TIME TO REST IS WHEN YOU DON'T THINK YOU CAN.

"Believe me, my young friend, there is nothing – absolutely nothing – half so much worth doing as simply messing about in boats."

"Why, there he is, the little fellow!"

NOTHING THAT MATTERS TO
US IS EVER TRULY LOST.

"Come along! Think of poor Otter, waiting up there by the ford!"

GOOD THINGS COME TO THOSE WHO WAIT.

"O, sir!" said Toad, crying afresh, "I am a poor unhappy washerwoman, and I've lost all my money, and can't pay for a ticket, and I must get home

to-night somehow, and whatever I am to do I don't know. O dear, O dear!!"

FAKE IT UNTIL YOU MAKE IT.

"In due time, we shall be home-sick once more for quiet water-lilies swaying on the surface of an English stream."

— THERE'S NOWHERE QUITE LIKE HOME.

"That was clove, that warm whiff on the breeze," the wayfarer remarked; "and those are cows we hear cropping the grass behind us. Everything seems asleep, and yet going on all the time. It is a goodly life that you lead, friend."

"Yes, it is the life, the only life to live," responded the Water Rat dreamily.

A LIFE LIVED AMONG NATURE IS
A LIFE WELL LIVED!

"I never stick too long to one ship."

THERE'S A BIG WORLD OUT THERE.
GO FORTH AND EXPLORE!

"For the days pass, and never return, and the South still waits for you. Take the Adventure, heed the call, now ere the irrevocable moment passes!"

THERE'S A BIG WORLD OUT THERE.
GO FORTH AND EXPLORE!

"For the days pass, and never return, and the South still waits for you. Take the Adventure, heed the call, now ere the irrevocable moment passes!"

DON'T HIDE,
WAITING FOR THE STORM TO PASS,
BUT PUT YOUR BEST FOOT FORWARD
AND WELCOME THE RAIN.

"I've an idea
that you'll feel
a lot better when
you've got
something
jotted down
– if it's only just
the rhymes."

WHEN YOUR THOUGHTS
BECOME TOO MANY,
TRY WRITING THEM
DOWN ON PAPER.

"I've heard that song before," said Toad, laughing as he continued to spur his steed onward in its wild career.

GO YOUR OWN WAY!

"Sit still, and you shall know what driving really is, for you are in the hands of the famous, the skilful, the entirely fearless Toad!"

BELIEF IN YOURSELF
WILL TAKE YOU ANYWHERE
YOU WANT TO GO.

"O Ratty!" Toad cried. "I've been through such times since I saw you last, you can't think! Such trials, such sufferings, and all so nobly borne!"

EVERYONE NEEDS A FRIEND SOMETIMES.

MR RAT
TRADESMENS
ENTRANCE
NO BOTTLES

"Quite right, Ratty!
How sound you always are!
Yes I've been a conceited old
ass, I can quite see that; but
now I'm going to be a good
Toad, and not do it any more."

TRUE COURAGE LIES
IN BEING ABLE TO
ADMIT OUR FAULTS
AND CONSTANTLY
STRIVE TO BE
BETTER.

"There, there!" went on the Badger more kindly. "Never mind. Stop crying. We're going to let bygones be bygones."

FORGIVENESS IS THE THREAD THAT
WILL MEND ANY FRIENDSHIP.

"Well, it's time we were all in bed."